LIBERATOR:
THE PEOPLE'S GUARD

CRAIG WEIDHUNER

Tellwell Talent
www.tellwell.ca

ISBN
978-0-2288-7909-1 (Hardcover)
978-0-2288-7911-4 (Paperback)
978-0-2288-7910-7 (eBook)

Volume 1:
State-Sponsored Hero

1

Location: City of Movogorsky, Democratic People's Republic of Ruthenia

Tovarich Revanov darted silently across the streets of Movogorsky, the capital city of the country of Ruthenia. It was the middle of the night, and the streets were deserted due to the cold of the autumn night and the state's strict curfew. Despite its name, the Democratic People's Republic of Ruthenia was neither democratic nor a republic of the people. It was a communist dictatorship. It happened approximately thirty years ago; Ruthenia, like many of the world's nations, was embroiled in a world war—a war that taxed Ruthenia's fragile industry and infrastructure. It didn't help that the war effort was being mismanaged due to government corruption and inefficiency. Fed up with such incompetence, the populace rose up, overthrew the government, and established a communist dictatorship. While they initially promised the people a fair and just society where the wealthy elite would no longer exploit the workers and peasants, this new government became the very thing they vowed to fight. Seizing control of all industry, the conditions of the workers did little to improve. The only real difference now was that if anyone complained, they were promptly arrested as "enemies of the people." This was why Tovarich was out on such a cold dark night—because those were the exact type of people he was secretly meeting with tonight. Tovarich had joined a secret group of dissidents calling themselves "the Nihilists." Their goal was to launch terrorist attacks against the government, the Communist Party of Ruthenia, to force them to accept liberal reforms. At least that's what the Nihilists believed. They didn't know that Tovarich Revanov was actually an agent of the Ruthenian secret police sent to infiltrate this group, learn everything he could about them, gain their trust, and lure them into a trap. Tovarich convinced them to meet tonight to prepare for a terrorist attack. While he was acting the part of a terrorist plotting to take down the government, he was actually wearing a hidden microphone. It allowed the secret police to hear everything, then move in so they could have them all arrested.

Tovarich was a young man in his late twenties. He had short blond hair hidden under his fur-lined cap. He had brown eyes that were cold and hard like steel, and he was dressed in a black and grey fur coat with heavy winter boots to help keep out the cold weather. Not that Tovarich was bothered by the weather, the only cold he felt was cold contempt for the terrorists he was secretly meeting. Having been born shortly after the communist party seized control of the country, he had grown up with the state's propaganda constantly drilled into his head. From the time he was a small child, he was taught that the communist party was the greatest gift Ruthenia had ever received—that they would deliver the people a socialist utopia where everyone would be equal, and there would be plenty of everything for everyone to share. He had been taught that the current hardships people faced were caused by the western capitalist nations like Usonia, plotting to destroy their socialist paradise out of jealousy. He was taught that all citizens must be ever vigilant against spies of "western imperialist" nations working to undermine everything that Ruthenia would achieve. Like all Ruthenians, he had been taught from a young age that "enemies of the people" don't deserve compassion or mercy—dogmatism that Tovarich took to heart. Ever since he was a child, he excelled in school. In elementary school, he could already read at a high school level. In gym class, he displayed the strength and stamina of a boy twice his age and in both history and Marxist philosophy, he soaked up information like a sponge. The state quickly saw great potential in this youth. Thus, they quickly recruited him into the secret police to mould him into the ideal agent who could be trusted to root out potential threats to the state before they even began.

Tovarich ran quickly between the buildings. Tovarich was careful to avoid being seen despite the streets being empty. He was playing the part of a terrorist, so he had to make it look as though he were trying to avoid drawing unwanted attention to himself, to help make himself look like one of the enemies of the state he had been taught to despise so much. Tovarich raced down a dark alley to a back door leading to a kitchen in a restaurant that was closed for the night. At least, it was closed to the public; tonight, the Nihilists were meeting here to discuss their terrorist attack. Tovarich knocked a specific rhythm on the door. The door opened a crack as someone peeked out to see who it was. Upon recognizing Tovarich, the man opened the door and ushered him inside.

The restaurant was dark, the only light coming from some small candles lit on a few tables. Sitting around the tables were the members of the Nihilists. They varied in age and gender, but they all had in common a burning hatred for the authoritarian government that ran the country. Taking their name from a movement over a hundred years ago, the Nihilists rejected the existing government order. While many had initially supported the communist party after it took control of the country, the state's increasingly repressive measures and constant surveillance of the populace led them to become disillusioned with the government. They initially started by publishing anti-government propaganda, to which the government responded by having their offices raided, their printing presses seized, and their publications banned as "fake news." Soon they found themselves being constantly monitored and harassed by the authorities in an attempt to shut them down. Ironically, all the state really did was drive them to take more extreme measures. First, it started with protests, later acts of sabotage against state-run industries, and eventually acts of domestic terrorism.

This is what led Tovarich to go undercover and infiltrate this organization. Between feeding them misinformation and even getting the authorities to look the other way occasionally, he had gained their trust. Now that he had convinced them all to meet with him in secret, the state was ready to pounce. Unknown to the Nihilists, dozens of secret police were surrounding the restaurant. Inside, Tovarich was stalling for time by laying out a fake plan to commit another terrorist attack.

A plan that Tovarich made sure would never come to fruition.

"...we'll sneak into government offices and start planting bombs," Tovarich told the others. He was trying to convince them to finally step out of hiding and let the country know who they were and what their goals were. "That will show the government that we're not going to sit silently while they control our lives!"

Some of the Nihilists nodded and murmured in agreement. A few were still not convinced.

"It's still too dangerous!" one of those few insisted. "If we're discovered, they'll execute us all."

"You would sit back and do nothing?" Tovarich asked. "You would sit silently and cower in fear while the state continues to oppress us?" He spoke with the passion and eloquence of a party member addressing a crowd to feed them state propaganda. "We won't take the government down with timid half measures. Only through bold action can we force the state to give in to our demands! We have to let them know that the people of Ruthenia won't be bullied by the state anymore!" Tovarich's words seemed to have roused the rest of the Nihilists, except for the lone individual who still felt it was too dangerous. However, given how the rest of the group had been swept up by Tovarich's rhetoric, he simply stood there silent.

Suddenly the restaurant's front door burst open, and dozens of armed secret police officers rushed in, guns drawn and aimed at the Nihilists. "FREEZE!" Yuri, the leader of the police troop, shouted, "YOU'RE ALL UNDER ARREST!"

"They found us!" Tovarich shouted with shock. "How is this possible?"

The lone Nihilist who still had his doubts glared at Tovarich, "Because *you* betrayed us!"

Tovarich turned to him with shock. "How could you say that? Wasn't I the one who was the most vocal about fighting back against the state? Wasn't I the one who proposed direct attacks against the government?"

"Which is exactly why you're the traitor," he pointed out. "You provided us with all the details, the intel, the equipment necessary. How else could you have gotten access to all of that? The only way was that you're an undercover agent, sent by the state to root us out. As for your eloquent speech, who else but an agent of the state would say such things? What better way to gain our trust than by acting like you hated the government so much? You won our trust by telling us exactly what we wanted to hear."

Tovarich just stood there silently. The jig was up. With his cover blown, Agent Yuri, Tovarich's close friend, saw no need to continue the charade, "Very well then," Yuri turned to Tovarich. "Agent

Tovarich Revanov, your service to the state is noted and greatly appreciated."

Tovarich smiled and nodded at Yuri. He then turned to face the rest of the Nihilists. His look changed to one of cold contempt, "Good night," was all he said before turning and walking out the door.

LOCATION: CENTRAL MEETING ROOM, THE CITADEL, MOVOGORSKY, PEOPLE'S REPUBLIC OF RUTHENIA

The Citadel was a large building located in the heart of the capital city of Movogorsky. It was both a fortress and a palace, and it was built several hundred years ago when the country was still an empire under the rule of the Tsar. After the communist party overthrew the government, it became the offices of the various members of the party. As a result, it was an odd mix of wealth and spartan simplicity. Such was the central meeting room where a top-secret meeting of the highest-ranking members of the communist party was currently being held.

The room was large and rather ornate for a communist party, with a large Persian rug spread across the floor under a large wooden table where the various members of the party sat. The room seemed more befitting of a board room of a large corporation. To some, it might have been decried as a symbol of capitalist wealth. While that might have been the party's official stance, many party members were known not to practice what they preached. They were more concerned about the average citizen living up to the ideals that the party members often failed to live up to themselves. But then again, why live up to your own example when you could simply have your critics silenced and labelled "enemies of the people." However, there was one exception: General Nikolai Duboshnev.

General Duboshnev was the commander of the Ruthenian Army and a high-ranking member of the communist party. He was originally a common soldier of the old republic until he defected and joined a group of rebels fighting to overthrow the government and establish the current Ruthenian communist republic. As a reward for his help in seizing power, he was promoted to the rank of General. As the years went on, his skill, intelligence, and political motivations enabled him to advance to a five-star General and assume direct command of the Ruthenian People's Army. It also made him a strong voice in the communist party, hence why he called a top-secret meeting of the central committee, meeting with other high-ranking members of the military, department of intelligence, and other politicians to discuss how to deal with growing dissidence and terrorist movements, such as the Nihilists.

"There's still the matter of growing dissident movements sweeping across the country," one of the party members protested. "Not to mention organized crime is still a growing problem in Ruthenia."

"I've given that plenty of thought," General Duboshnev reassured him.

"What is your plan, General?" another member of the party asked. "Crushing them with military force has proven ineffective."

"Which is why we need another way. We need to regain the support of the people," he explained. "We need to create a symbol for people to look up to. We need a state-sponsored hero."

The various members of the committee murmured amongst each other. There had been reports of unregistered superheroes from various nations worldwide: masked/costumed vigilantes helping to fight crime. To prevent such vigilantes from taking the law into their own hands, many nations began creating registration programs for these so-called superheroes. These registered or "state-sponsored heroes" were like a cross between the military and the police. They were employed by their nation's governments, given costumes and code names (while their true identities became classified), and sent out on missions to help fight crime and protect the innocent. In many ways, they had the same authority as the police.

"Are you proposing that we bring back the people's guard? The hero code-named Liberator?" one of the committee members asked, slightly nervous.

"I am," Duboshnev confirmed.

"But the Liberator was 'retired' from service almost thirty years ago," another member pointed out.

"Which is why now is the right time to bring him back," Duboshnev said. "A new people's guard for a new generation. Someone to take up the mantle of his predecessor."

The other committee members muttered amongst each other uneasily, "Considering what happened last time, are you sure this is a good idea?" one of them asked.

"I assure you, the mistakes of his predecessor won't burden this new one," Duboshnev replied. "I've been working on an improved version of the formula we used before."

"Need I remind you of what happened to the previous test subjects, General?" one of the ministers spoke up. "There's a reason we destroyed the evidence and classified the project top-secret."

"I assure you that we've improved the formula; we won't have any mistakes this time," General Duboshnev replied confidently.

"How can you be sure?"

Duboshnev answered his question by going into a rather lengthy explanation of the whole process.

He deliberately used complicated scientific terms and in-depth technical explanations combined with scientific formulas and mathematical equations. The truth is, Duboshnev didn't think much of his fellow ministers. He held most of them in contempt as he viewed them as inferior both physically and mentally. He figured if he gave them a long and complicated response, they'd get lost in all the technobabble, get bored, and eventually give up.

The various ministers let out exasperated sighs. They knew it was pointless to continue discussing the matter. Most of them had little to no expertise in biology or genetics. Some of them figured Duboshnev was doing this purposely. One of Duboshnev's skills was patience. He knew he could spend hours, if necessary, going over every little detail, repeatedly if necessary. Finally, one of the ministers raised his hand, telling Duboshnev to stop. "Very well, General, you've made your point," he sighed. "Whom did you have in mind to become our new Liberator?"

"I've decided that Tovarich Revanov would be an excellent candidate," Duboshnev replied proudly. "He's strong, he's intelligent, and he's extremely loyal to the state. He's the perfect candidate."

Most of the other ministers murmured and nodded in agreement.

LOCATION: GENERAL DUBOSHNEV'S OFFICE, THE CITADEL, MOVOGORSKY

General Duboshnev's office was small and spartan in its simplicity compared to the meeting room where he met with the other party members just a few hours earlier. It consisted of a simple wooden desk with three wooden chairs—two for whomever he was meeting and a third he was currently sitting behind going over various reports. The only other objects in his office were a computer and a small desk lamp in the corner of the desk. Beyond that, his office was only adorned with a metal filing cabinet near the left wall and a specially commissioned painting of Duboshnev, along with great communist leaders of the past, hanging on the wall to the right. Duboshnev was a man who didn't outright despise material wealth, but at the same time, he saw no need to show it off. He preferred to let his actions and deeds show off his greatness, not works of art or expensive/lavish furnishings.

Despite being in his late fifties, the General still cut an imposing figure. Even under his military uniform, adorned with various medals, he was still a well-muscled figure who arguably could take on and defeat a man half his age in a fight. Aside from his once dark brown hair, now mostly grey, his appearance made him look as though he were ten years younger. He was sitting at his desk signing various reports when a knock came at the door.

"Come in," General Duboshnev called out.

The door opened, and Tovarich walked in, "You wanted to see me, sir."

"Yes, Tovarich, come in. Please sit down," he said, motioning Tovarich to one of the chairs facing his desk. Tovarich nodded respectfully and sat down. Tovarich had great respect for General Duboshnev. He was the closest thing Tovarich had to a father. Tovarich never knew his father; according to everyone, his father was a loyal factory worker who sacrificed his life to save his fellow employees from a horrific workplace accident while Tovarich's mother was still pregnant with him. Growing up without a father, Duboshnev took him under his wing. He always watched out for him, occasionally helped raise him, and taught him much about life. In many ways, Tovarich thought of Nikolai Duboshnev as his father.

"First, I want to congratulate and thank you for your work in apprehending those terrorists," Duboshnev smiled.

Tovarich shrugged, "I was just doing my duty as a loyal citizen of the state."

Duboshnev chuckled, "You're too humble, Tovarich."

"You were the one who always told me it's not about fame or glory," Tovarich reminded him, "it's about doing what's best for the people, even if they don't realize it. What was it you always said? 'When you give people a choice, sometimes they'll make the wrong choice, so it's up to us to make the right choices for them.'"

Hearing Tovarich repeat his words filled Duboshnev with pride; he taught him well. "I'm glad to hear that, Tovarich. I've watched you ever since you were a little boy, and I always knew you'd grow into a valuable citizen of the state. Which is why I've chosen you for a special project." He slid a folder with "TOP SECRET" stamped on it.

Tovarich took the folder, opened it, and read the papers inside.

"You're familiar with the people's guard, I assume," the General stated. "Our once great hero named 'Liberator.'"

"I remember vaguely," Tovarich nodded.

The Liberator, also known as "the people's guard," was the original registered superhero of the Democratic People's Republic of Ruthenia. He was named "Liberator" because he would liberate the workers and peasants of Ruthenia from the hardships suffered under their "imperialist overlords" and guard and protect them from western imperialist powers that threatened to destroy their communist society. Hence why he also had the nickname "the people's guard." The

Liberator served the state before Tovarich was born. According to the stories he'd been told as a child, the Liberator heroically sacrificed his life to protect the country from terrorists plotting to unleash a deadly virus upon the country. The Liberator defeated these terrorists, destroying their base and their virus at the cost of his own life. At the time, the state decided to retire him as they felt there was no one worthy of continuing the legacy of the people's guard.

"We'd like you to be the new Liberator," Duboshnev told Tovarich.

"ME?" Tovarich was genuinely shocked by the news. "I'm no Liberator," he insisted. As a child, Tovarich looked up to the Liberator. He recalled how he'd often tie a bath towel around his neck like a cape and run around his apartment, pretending to be the Liberator, fighting crime and being a great hero. He never imagined that he'd actually get the chance to live out his childhood fantasy one day.

"You feel it's impossible to live up to his standards?" Duboshnev asked. As a child, Tovarich heard many stories about the Liberator and his almost superhuman abilities: possessing strength, stamina, and agility beyond an ordinary man. As he got older, Tovarich simply assumed these were simply myths and exaggerations of his abilities. Duboshnev knew this from various talks he had with Tovarich over the years. "You think all those stories about him being stronger, faster, and smarter than the average person was just state propaganda? What if I told you the stories were all true?"

"How is that possible? Are you going to tell me he had some sort of 'mystical force?'" Tovarich replied doubtfully. He heard rumours about beings with a "mystical force," whether it be magical essence, demonic aura, or spiritual powers. He heard that some people felt such powers were "unnatural" and that beings such as demons and mages were forced to live in secret, hiding from the rest of the world to avoid being persecuted. However, Tovarich dismissed such rumours as the works of people with an overactive imagination.

"Read on," Duboshnev motioned toward the rest of the papers in the folder.

Tovarich continued reading through the papers, "A *'metamorphic human'*...super formula...genetic re-coding...DNA re-sequencing?" Tovarich read through the reports about a secret project called "The Metamorphosis Directive"—a secret project by a group of ambitious scientists to create a new breed of humans, physically stronger, mentally superior, resistant to disease, allergies and other ailments that affected regular humans. He looked up at General Duboshnev and said, "I've never heard about this...project."

"I'm not surprised," Duboshnev replied. "It was a secret project by a group of ambitious scientists working without the knowledge or consent of the world's governments. When the world's various governments found out, they sent a covert team to shut down the project. They hid all knowledge of the project from the world."

"Why?" Tovarich asked.

"I think you already know the reason," Duboshnev replied.

Tovarich nodded.

If word of this had gotten out, it would have caused a massive scandal. Governments would have instantly accused one another of being responsible for this, which would have reignited old prejudices. Accusations of "tampering with the laws of nature/of God" and dividing the people of the world—an "our kind versus their kind" scenario. However, it did bring another unpleasant thought to Tovarich's mind. "What about when the other nations of the world find out? What would they say if they knew Ruthenia was attempting to re-create metamorphic humans?" he asked.

Duboshnev countered, "You don't think other nations like Usonia or the Republic of Prussia aren't already doing the same?"

"They are?" Tovarich asked with genuine surprise.

Duboshnev nodded. "The Metamorphosis Directive was an independent project; they answered to no one. You know how governments are; they only object to such projects when they're *not* the ones carrying them out. It's always the same old story: 'It's only wrong when *you* do it! When we do it, it's okay.' We're only ensuring that we're levelling the playing field."

Tovarich understood, "Like the nuclear arms race. Our nukes are only there to ensure that the other side doesn't do something foolish with theirs."

"Exactly," Duboshnev explained. "Remember your early teachings, Tovarich: 'It's the responsibility of the state to protect the people from the threats of western imperialists who wish to destroy our socialist utopia.'"

"To prevent our ideas of fairness and equality from spreading to their nations. Otherwise, their workers would rise up against their oppressors." Tovarich recalled his early indoctrination into the teachings of communist philosophy. "I understand. If it helps protect the state and its people, I'll do it."

Duboshnev smiled, "I knew I could count on you, Tovarich."

LOCATION: CLASSIFIED (TOP-SECRET MEDICAL LABORATORY)

The next day, Tovarich reported to the medical laboratory to begin the procedure. It was small and seemed to be a cross between a medical facility and a gym. In the middle of the room was a gurney with a small table on wheels to its left. On the table was a metal tray with various medical syringes, which contained the formula that would enable Tovarich to become the Liberator. To the right of the gurney was a portable computer to monitor Tovarich's vitals. Before being administered the formula, he was ordered to perform a few tests of his physical abilities as a baseline for comparison. The tests were being overseen by two of Ruthenia's most brilliant scientific minds, doctor Pavel Alexandrovich Ulyanov and doctor Petro Volkov. Pavel was about the same age as Tovarich. He was slightly taller and more slender with short curly brown hair and brown eyes that sat behind a pair of glasses. Unlike Tovarich, Pavel wasn't as muscular; his strongest muscle was his brain. He was quite analytical, able to think outside the box, and was a quick learner. This was why the Ruthenian government had recruited him into their scientific division. They saw his intellect as both a blessing and a threat; a blessing in that it would prove quite useful to them under their control and a threat in that if they didn't watch over him, he might have put his intellect to uses that could prove dangerous to the communist party's iron grip on the country. In a totalitarian state, nothing was more dangerous than a person who could think for themselves. Pavel was aware of this; thus, he acquiesced to their demands as it was better than finding himself arrested as a potential enemy of the state.

For Petro, it was much the same story: a gifted intellectual who was recruited by the state to ensure he wouldn't end up using his intellect against them. Petro was a slender man with short blond hair and hazel eyes. Like Pavel, he was also a man who was more brain than brawn. Both had been fortunate in that they could convince the state that they were of more use to Ruthenia as scientists in a lab than as soldiers in the military. Thus, they were a few of the fortunate individuals that managed to avoid mandatory military service, even though they were indirectly serving the military in performing the procedure that would turn Tovarich into the next Liberator.

First, they took his pulse and blood pressure and then had him perform some weightlifting using an exercise bench and a set of barbells. Having served in the military and his combat training as a secret police officer, Tovarich was already considerably strong. He could easily lift over 200 kg and repeat this long after others would have been forced to stop due to fatigue. Next, they had him run on a treadmill. Again, he ran with speed and endurance that would have made an Olympic athlete envious. In fact, Tovarich had been considered for the Ruthenian Olympic team. The only reason he hadn't been recruited was due to Tovarich and General Duboshnev convincing the state that his talents were better served in other ways than winning medals. Next came a series of intelligence tests. Said tests showed not only that Tovarich had an above-average intelligence but also a keen analytical mind with the ability to learn and adapt quickly. Finally, they performed various medical examinations, blood tests, urine samples, and other examinations. When it was over, Tovarich sat on the gurney while Pavel read the test results.

"Your blood pressure is normal and your pulse is actually lower than average, meaning your heart is in excellent shape," Pavel explained as he read the various charts. "Strength and stamina is well above average. Lung efficiency is about fifty percent stronger than average. If only we were all in as good shape as you are."

Tovarich laughed it off, "I guess I don't need this formula after all. Maybe *you* should take it instead." Tovarich paused as he reflected upon his words, "I'm sorry, Doctor Ulyanov. I didn't mean..."

"It's all right," Pavel cut him off, "I know it wasn't meant as an insult. You were chosen for a reason, probably because they figured if we can enhance the best of the best, then..."

Tovarich nodded. Pavel didn't need to finish. Tovarich assumed that Pavel and Petro had been informed about the Metamorphosis Directive. Although the project was officially classified,

Tovarich figured that they would have been informed about it to replicate the results. With all their tests completed, the procedure commenced. It was simple: a series of injections designed to alter Tovarich's DNA slightly to overcome the built-in natural limitations of the human body. Theoretically, this would allow Tovarich to push himself beyond the limits of what was normally considered possible for humans and ensure that his body and mind would have their abilities greatly enhanced. Ironically, the results of the tests Tovarich had already performed would seem to imply that he was already beyond peak performance. They couldn't help but wonder how such genetic modifications would enhance Tovarich even greater than he already was.

After the procedure was completed, Tovarich was left to rest while he was hooked up to the medical computer to monitor his vital signs. His pulse, blood pressure, and blood oxygen levels didn't appear to change. Tovarich spent the night in the lab being monitored around the clock. The following morning, Pavel and Petro examined him again to compare the results with their earlier tests. Tovarich went through the exact same tests he did the day before. This time, the results were even more impressive: Tovarich lifted the same sets of 200kg weights as if they were made of plastic and hollow. Similarly, he set a new speed record when running on the treadmill.

"Impressive," Pavel noted. "In your current state, I think you'd beat me in a race if I were in a car." Tovarich kept running; he had been at it for over an hour and still didn't feel tired. "You can stop now," Pavel told him. "I'd say the formula worked perfectly."

2

LOCATION: TOVARICH'S APARTMENT, CITY OF MOVOGORSKY

It had been a year since Tovarich had been genetically enhanced and assumed the role of the new Liberator. With the results of the experiment declared a success, OPERATION LIBERATOR was now in full swing. As the Liberator, he now wore a modified version of the original outfit worn by his predecessor. It was red with yellow tights over the top to match the colours of the nation's flag. He had yellow boots and gloves, a yellow cape, and a red bandana/mask that covered his head completely, going down to his nose with two eye holes allowing him to see. Emblazoned across the chest was a large yellow star.

Tovarich had hoped that as the Liberator, he could use his new powers to better serve the people.

He hoped he would continue his work as a secret agent, rooting out dissidents and other potential threats to the state. He soon discovered that the state had other plans for him. He had become the new symbol of the Democratic People's Republic of Ruthenia. He was the state's new hero and mascot, and the state was eager to promote him. Thus, the Liberator was sent around the country to give patriotic speeches, march in parades, and engage in other forms of publicity. The government also began mass production of Liberator merchandise. Tovarich found it strange that the state would engage in such "greedy capitalist behaviour," as he had always been taught. It seemed like a slap in the face to everything their communist "utopia" was supposed to stand for. Tovarich was quickly learning that it wasn't only the western powers that didn't practice what they preached. His own government, despite its constant messages of the "evils of mass consumerism," had no problem using it to serve their own ends. The government justified it by saying that since the state owned every industry and retailer in the country, all the money was being funnelled back into the state rather than the private coffers of the wealthy elite, like in the west. There was all manner of merchandise of the Liberator. Everything from posters to action figures to children's costumes. Bookstores began carrying Liberator comics and novels, all telling various fictional stories where he would use his "communist" powers to defeat various capitalist-themed villains planning to destroy the country with their "sinister" plots to introduce freedom of speech, run their own business for profit, and teach people not to follow the will of the state blindly. They even made an animated series based on him.

Tovarich sat in his apartment watching his TV series, *The Adventures of the Liberator*. Tovarich took another swig from the half-empty bottle of vodka. He couldn't believe what he was watching. It was a cartoon version of himself. They tried to get Tovarich to voice his animated counterpart, but Tovarich was no actor. Instead, a professional voice actor was hired to voice him. Tovarich's role was limited to a brief live-action scene at the end of each episode, where he would stare directly into the camera to deliver a patriotic message to the audience. In this episode, the Liberator's teenage sidekick, Peasant Boy, had been captured by his "arch-nemesis," the Republican, a villain based on right-wing Usonian politicians. He was dressed in a garish red and white striped suit with dark blue patches and white stars as if someone cut up the flag of Usonia and turned it into a suit. He had Peasant Boy tied to a nuclear missile and was about to launch it. The Republican was busy hamming it up, giving a monologue about his evil scheme for the episode.

"...and so when the missile launches, you'll leave a lasting impression on the Citadel!" The Republican laughed maniacally. "Unfortunately for you and the rest of your government, none of you will be left alive!" The Republican then proceeded to cackle wildly.

"You'll never get away with this!" Peasant Boy yelled defiantly.

"Really, and who exactly is going to stop me?" the Republican scoffed.

"That would be me, you sinister fiend!" the animated Liberator shouted as he burst into the room.

The Republican turned in shock. "Impossible! You can't be alive!"

"I escaped your little trap, Republican," the Liberator boasted in an over-the-top manner. "However, you won't escape prison! Now come along quietly!"

"NEVER!" the Republican shouted. "ATTACK!" he called out to his henchmen.

Tovarich took another swig from his bottle. He rolled his eyes, watching as his television counterpart engaged in a fistfight with the Republican's henchmen. Being a former soldier trained in hand-to-hand combat, Tovarich couldn't help but feel contempt for the show depicting the fight in such a ridiculous manner. Both his character and the villains took such wide, clumsy swings. It didn't help that the fight scene was punctuated with comic book-style captions. Whenever someone hit someone else, the words "BAM," "POW," "Oooof," and so on would flash across the screen. Tovarich finished off the last of his vodka and turned the TV off. He couldn't help but imagine that if that scene had been real—that had he really been there fighting such villains with his military combat training— he would have easily dispatched them all in a matter of seconds. When Tovarich saw the first rough cut of this series, he pointed out its various flaws; the tone and writing all seemed so campy and ridiculous that he couldn't believe anyone would take it seriously. It seemed more like they were mocking him. When he complained to the ministry in charge of broadcasting, they simply told him realism wasn't important; the goal of the series was to indoctrinate future Ruthenians with communist philosophy. Thus, the Liberator of the series came across as an invincible hero who could do no wrong. Conversely, the villains of the series came across as clichéd, committing crime for no other reason than because it was the "evil" thing to do, even when said "evil" deeds proved to be a hindrance to their own plans. Tovarich couldn't help but notice that if anyone in the series actually acted with some shred of intelligence, the plot of the episode would have been resolved in five minutes.

Meanwhile, elsewhere in Movogorsky, in a secret bunker, another man was also watching the series—a mysterious man who preferred to simply go by the name "the Intellectual." He was a lanky man in his mid-thirties. He had short, messy black hair and hazel eyes that seemed to stare wildly, almost aimlessly. What he lacked in impressive physical abilities and appearance, he more than made up for in mental abilities. This was why he went by the name "the Intellectual." He had a razor-sharp mind with keen analytical abilities. He prided himself on his ability to anticipate any and every possible outcome. Like Tovarich, he, too, was watching the show in complete disbelief at the over-the-top nature of the series. Unlike Tovarich, his discontent came from the fact that the Liberator and the Ruthenian government, by extension, came across as the heroes. As far as he was concerned, the communist party was the real villain of the story. Thus, as the episode ended with the Liberator saving Peasant Boy, defeating the Republican, and "making the planet safe for the workers of the world," the Intellectual also rolled his eyes. The episode ended with a brief scene of the real Liberator, standing in front of a giant flag of the People's Republic, waving proudly in the breeze. The Liberator stood there giving a rousing, if not patronizing, speech to young viewers about how good citizens never question the state, have unwavering faith in the government, and so on. The Intellectual wasn't listening; the actual words weren't important. It didn't matter what the Liberator said; the basic message was one of blind obedience to the government. The Intellectual turned off the TV just as one of his followers entered the room.

"If only the real government were as pathetic and incompetent as their animated counterparts," the Intellectual said, "they would never have been able to have my Nihilists arrested." For it was the Intellectual who had founded and was the leader of this group. Allowing a spy for the government into his organization to infiltrate and have several of his followers arrested filled him with even more contempt for the state and for the Liberator in particular. In truth, he was disappointed in himself for not foreseeing such an event. The Intellectual took the name as a way to mock the state, which claimed intellectuals such as himself were a threat to the state because they dared to be better than the people. However he had to admit that it was partially true. The Intellectual saw himself as smarter than other people. That's why he formed the Nihilists. Despite the constant propaganda, he saw the government for what they really were: a group of self-righteous, power-hungry bureaucrats. Despite their claims of building a socialist utopia, their real goal was nothing more than holding onto complete power at all costs. In many ways, they really weren't that different from the right-wing politicians of the west they constantly criticized. The Intellectual thought himself to be better and smarter than them. He prided himself on anticipating every possible outcome; thus, he didn't like it when he "miscalculated," such as when he failed to see Tovarich arresting his followers.

"What'll we do next, sir?" his follower asked, snapping the Intellectual back to reality.

"Don't interrupt me when I'm thinking!" the Intellectual barked. He didn't like it when someone derailed his train of thoughts.

"Sorry, boss," his follower responded sheepishly.

The Intellectual stood up, "Fortunately, I always have contingency plans. Next Tuesday is 'Liberation Day,'" he reminded his follower. It was a national holiday celebrating the communist government overthrowing the country's old government, 'liberating' the people from the shackles of the old state, ending the last world war, and bringing the citizens of Ruthenia the 'great gift of this socialist paradise.' "I've got a plan to take care of both the Liberator and the Ruthenian government."

LOCATION: REVOLUTIONARY SQUARE, OUTSIDE THE CITADEL, MOVOGORSKY, RUTHENIA

Liberation day dawned bright and sunny. It was a perfect day to go outside and enjoy the warm spring weather. The city was abuzz in preparation for the celebration of being "liberated" by the communist government when they overthrew the old government almost thirty years ago. Buildings all over the city were draped with large red banners displaying images of great communist leaders of the past, standing tall and proud alongside images of the Liberator. Some banners had large slogans like "Long Live Communism" or "All Glory to the Soviets" written on them. In Revolutionary Square, the large paved plaza directly in front of the Citadel, preparations were underway for the military parade that was scheduled to take place that afternoon. A large stand with a podium was being erected directly in front of the Citadel, where the Premier and other important officials would stand delivering a speech touting all the glories of the state. On the other end of the plaza, barricades were being erected to hold back the throngs of excited crowds, specifically chosen for their loyalty to the state, who earned the honour of attending. Those deemed especially patriotic were given the distinction of being permitted to march in the parade waving large red flags, a symbol of the revolution, before rows of tanks and other military vehicles would roll past the Citadel in a display of the country's military might.

While everyone seemed to be getting ready for the day's events, one individual had no interest in such a spectacle, Doctor Pavel Ulyanov. To him, it was nothing more than a further reminder that all of them were essentially prisoners of the communist state. Of course, he knew better than to say such things out loud. Thus, he retreated to the sanctuary of his lab, where he was working when Petro walked in. "Aren't you going to the parade?" he asked.

"I'm very busy working on an experiment," Pavel replied.

"What kind of experiment?" Petro raised his eye suspiciously.

Pavel sighed, "All right, I'm not really working on anything," he confessed. "I just don't want to attend. I have no interest in watching the state parade around a bunch of tanks and weapons. What do they need me there for anyway?"

"I understand," Petro replied sympathetically. "Unfortunately, we have orders from the Central Committee. We have to attend whether we want to or not."

Pavel let out a dejected sigh and slowly stood up, "I suppose so." And he wasn't the only one.

***

The Liberator was sitting in a chair while other soldiers raced around, making sure all their military equipment looked spotless while waiting for the parade to start. the Liberator, on the other hand, was killing time drawing on a notepad. He sketched a picture of himself as a circus monkey in his costume, performing for the amusement of the crowd. The sound of footsteps approaching made him stop. Placing his drawing face-down so that no one would see it, he saw General Duboshnev walking toward him. The Liberator stood at attention as the General approached.

"At ease," Duboshnev said.

The Liberator nodded and relaxed.

"It's time," Duboshnev told him.

"Yes, sir," he replied. As he prepared, Duboshnev bent down and picked up the drawing Tovarich had been working on. Tovarich felt a sense of unease as Duboshnev studied the picture. Duboshnev looked up at him.

"The Liberator, trained monkey? Performing the tricks that entertain the crowds?" Duboshnev asked with a slightly humorous tone.

Tovarich let out a sigh of relief. He was worried Duboshnev might misinterpret such work as a sign of subversive behaviour. He should have known Duboshnev was more understanding than that. "I must confess, sir, that I'm not very keen about being put on display like this. I feel like my talents are being wasted. After all, what was the point of genetically enhancing me if all I'm supposed to do is march in parades and sell Liberator merchandise? Anyone can do that."

Duboshnev gently placed his hand on the Liberator's shoulder, "Remember, Tovarich, part of your duty as the Liberator is to be a symbol to the people. I understand the way you feel. I sympathize, but the best way to fight off the capitalists is by rousing the people's patriotic feelings to show them that the state, like you, is invincible."

Tovarich was still upset, but he realized the General was right. "Of course, I understand. Our number one duty is always to the state. It's the right thing to do."

"I'm glad to hear that," Duboshnev smiled. "Be patient, Tovarich. One day, you'll be able to do more than simply smile and wave to the crowds. I promise you that." And with that, General Duboshnev departed for the Citadel to take his place among the other dignitaries while Liberator prepared for his part in the parade to commence.

***

That afternoon, as the sun shone brightly on Revolutionary Square, the parade began. Throngs of loyal workers marched waving red flags, followed by military troops in their finest dress uniforms, their polished machine guns glistening in the sun. They turned and saluted the Premier and other government officials who stood there saluting back as they passed the platform. On the other side of the square, behind barricades and rows of heavily armed police, crowds of onlookers cheered and waved red flags. After the troops, a squad of military bands came by, marching and playing revolutionary tunes. Finally, the moment everyone was waiting for arrived. The Liberator marched down the middle of the square, turning and saluting the members of government and the crowd of cheering fans. Following the Liberator were rows of tanks rolling along as yet another symbol of the country's military might.

Those unable to attend in person watched the event on TV. Not that most people had a choice, it was the only program being broadcast on the state channel. Television sets across the country were filled with images of excited crowds cheering and waving red flags as the Liberator, followed by rows of tanks, rolled past the government officials.

The Premier of Ruthenia walked up to the podium. He stood there for a moment, smiling and waving at the enthusiastic crowds, cheering and waving red flags. Some of the crowd were genuinely excited, while others were faking it out of fear of being arrested for not showing enough support for the state. As the Premier spoke, all eyes were on him; only a select few had their attention elsewhere. The Liberator specifically focused on the rows of tanks in front of the Premier. He noticed them turning their guns and taking aim at the Premier. The Premier didn't seem to notice; he was too busy going on about how great their nation was and how their military would bring about world peace by crushing all hostile nations, enemies of the people, and so on. However, looking at the tanks, the Liberator felt something else was about to be crushed. He turned and raced toward the podium.

"GET DOWN!" the Liberator shouted and tackled the Premier, knocking him to the ground. The Liberator got to him just in time. No sooner were they lying on the ground did a tank shell sail over their heads, hitting the Citadel. Meanwhile, television sets across the country showed the whole event live to the Ruthenian people. Some watched with shock, some with horror, others with excitement. Whether they loved or feared what was happening, millions of citizens were glued to their TVs, watching and waiting to see what would happen next. Unfortunately for them, they wouldn't get to find out. The order came down from the government to cut the signal. Thus, millions of Ruthenians watched as their screens suddenly went blank with only plain white text reading, "Technical difficulties, please stand by."

Back at the Citadel, the Liberator ran toward the tank that fired the shot. He jumped on top of it, opened the hatch, and yanked the soldier out. "What do you think you're doing?" he barked.

"It wasn't me, I swear!" the soldier frantically insisted. As if to prove his point, the tank fired another shell at the Citadel. Hordes of people panicked and fled as debris came crashing down around them. The Liberator realized the soldier he was still holding was telling the truth. No one was operating the gun, yet it seemed to be acting on its own. He figured someone was remotely hacking the controls.

He put the soldier down. "See if you can regain control of the tank. Do whatever you can to stop it! Rip the wires and circuits out if you have to!" the Liberator ordered, then leapt from the tank toward the various politicians and military brass, desperately trying to avoid both being shot and crushed by falling debris. General Duboshnev stood there in shock; he hadn't anticipated his own tanks turning against him. Out of the corner of his eye, the Liberator saw one of the tanks aiming directly at the General. Turning toward the tank, the Liberator ran faster than ever before. The formula he'd been given had greatly enhanced his already impressive speed; he was gambling that it had done the same to his strength. Jumping into the tank with relative ease, he grabbed the barrel and began pulling, trying to aim it away from General Duboshnev. General Duboshnev watched in amazement. The Liberator was able to bend the barrel of the main gun, curving it upwards to a forty-five-degree angle. Even Pavel and Petro, standing in the crowd, watched in amazement. They knew the formula they had given him would enhance his natural abilities; however, they hadn't anticipated they would be improved this much.

"Come on," Pavel grabbed Petro and yanked him away. "Someone's obviously hacked the tanks' controls. Let's get back to the lab. Maybe we can find a way to stop them, shut them down."

"Right," Petro agreed, and the two of them ran off back to their lab.

General Duboshnev, the Premier, and other top-ranking officials watched in astonishment. Like Pavel and Petro, they expected that the formula would enhance his strength and stamina, though even they hadn't anticipated it would be by this much. According to their reports, his physical strength should have been about five times that of an ordinary man.

Meanwhile, another tank turned its main gun, aimed directly at the Liberator and fired. The explosion blasted the bent barrel and the Liberator clean off the tank. The force of the explosion should have killed him, yet it simply flung him into the wall. He hit it with such an impact that every bone in his body should have been shattered. Instead, he simply found himself lying on his back in the gaping hole now in the wall of the Citadel. It took Tovarich a minute to register what just happened. He looked up to see another tank barreling down on him. Instinctively, he put his hands up in an attempt to stop it. The tank simply rolled over him, smashing through the wall before coming to a stop directly on top of the Liberator.

General Duboshnev and the others simply stood there, jaws hanging from their mouths. Duboshnev's heart sank to his stomach. Not only had all their work in bringing back the Liberator been for nothing, but Tovarich, the young man whom the General had taken under his wing, whom he had watched over and mentored since he was a boy, was now dead. *No one, not even the Liberator, could have survived that*, he thought ruefully. He still recalled when the original Liberator had been killed. When it happened, he had been a young man, and now he was forced to watch history repeat itself.

"General," one of his aides shouted, "we need to get to the shelter; it's not safe here!"

His words and the sounds of more tank shells exploding snapped him back to the present. "Of course, Lieutenant," the General replied, regaining his composure. The General, the Premier, and the others rushed inside the Citadel, heading straight toward the secret bunker located deep beneath it and built to withstand even a nuclear attack. They made it inside just in time. Two junior officers closed the doors behind them but no sooner were they closed when a tank shell blasted them open. The General, the Premier, and the other top officials turned around. There was now a gaping hole where the front doors used to be. Mutilated body parts of what used to be the two junior officers were now scattered across the room. *Whoever is responsible for this will pay!* Duboshnev thought.

LOCATION: CENTRAL COMPUTER ROOM, CITADEL

Pavel and Petro returned to the central computer room located inside the Citadel. Normally, this room was used to monitor online communications across the country, to keep an eye out for potential online threats to the state—threats ranging from outsiders trying to hack government systems and gain access to classified materials to monitoring and taking down posts on social media that were critical of the government. Ironically, Pavel and Petro were here to try and hack the computer controls for the tanks and shut them down remotely. Pavel sat down at one of the computers. As a tech expert, part of his duties was to monitor all technical systems and make the necessary repairs, not to mention help design the software used in most government computer programs. Since he helped design most of the software used, he knew all the tricks necessary to access even restricted systems and files. Ordinarily, this would make him a potential threat to the state himself; however, he also knew the various tricks to ensure anything he did would be erased, thus making it virtually impossible for the state to track him. This was what he was doing right now, accessing classified files to find out how to take control of the tanks and stop them.

"Just as I suspected," Pavel said, "someone hacked into the tanks' systems and is controlling them remotely."

"Who?" asked Petro.

"I'm not sure," Pavel answered, feverishly typing away. "Help me find a way to stop it!" Petro sat down at another computer terminal next to Pavel. The two of them quickly raced against the clock, trying to find a way to regain control of the tanks and stop whoever was using them from attacking. They hoped that if they could figure out how someone managed to hack the tanks' controls remotely, they could use the same trick to wrest control back and stop the rampage. The low rumble of shells exploding further motivated them to find a solution before it was too late. While the computer lab was deep enough in the Citadel that there was little worry about their room taking a direct hit from a shell, they had no wish to end up trapped inside due to the surrounding rooms being reduced to piles of rubble. Thus, the two of them frantically searched through the computer network, looking for any malware or unusual programs that might account for what was happening. After searching for several minutes, Pavel found the program. "Hey, Petro, look at this."

LOCATION: REVOLUTIONARY SQUARE, OUTSIDE THE CITADEL, MOVOGORSKY, RUTHENIA

Outside, the tanks continued their rampage. Blasting away at the Citadel, gradually chipping away at brick and mortar. The Citadel was huge and spread over almost 300,000 square meters; thus, the tanks would exhaust their weapon supplies long before the whole structure collapsed. The soldiers inside the tank had no intention to continue attacking their own government with their military vehicles. If nothing else, they hoped their efforts to stop the attack would show the government that they weren't traitors who'd be blamed for this attack. The penalty for such an act of treason would be death. Thus, the soldiers worked frantically, trying anything to shut their tanks down. As the Liberator said, some of them even tried ripping out the wires and circuits in a desperate hope it might shut them down. However, despite their efforts, nothing seemed to make a difference. Fortunately, while they were ripping out the hardware, Pavel and Petro were hard at work in the computer lab, dismantling the foreign software someone installed into the tanks' computer systems. Thus, the soldiers and a few remaining civilians all breathed a collective sigh of relief as the tanks finally shut down.

* * *

Later, the survivors stood around surveying the damage. They looked at where the tank had run over the Liberator. They gathered around, assuming he was dead. Metamorphic-Human or not, there was no way anyone could have survived being run over by a tank.

General Duboshnev lowered his head sombrely. "Forgive me, Tovarich," he whispered.

"What shall we do now, General?" the Premier asked.

"We'll have to find a new Liberator," he answered glumly. "We must make sure the public doesn't know about this. We should tell them that he's been taken to the hospital and was seriously injured but still alive. That way, while we're searching for a new one, the public will simply believe he's recuperating."

"And when the people ask why he looks and sounds different?" another General asked.

"He had reconstructive surgery," Duboshnev explained. "The public needs to be reassured that the Liberator, like our nation, can recover from any tragedy and return stronger than ever."

The Premier was about to speak when grunting and groaning sounds coming from underneath the tank caught everyone's attention. They turned to see the tank slowly get pushed to the side. From underneath the treads, the Liberator crawled out. His costume was torn and covered with dirt, just like the exposed parts of his flesh. Surprisingly, he showed no signs of bruises or lacerations. Everyone stood there, jaws hanging open. The Liberator slowly got to his feet and staggered over to the crowd of gasping onlookers.

"He's still alive!"

"No one could have survived that!"

"How is this even possible?"

"It's a miracle!"

General Duboshnev walked over to the Liberator. Reaching out, he helped stabilize him, letting Tovarich lean on him for support. "You're alive," the General smiled.

The Liberator wearily nodded. He didn't feel it was necessary to respond to such a blatantly obvious statement.

"How is that possible?" the Premier asked.

"I don't know," the Liberator confessed. "When I was trying to resist the force of the tank pushing against me, it seemed like..." he shrugged, unable to find the proper words to describe it. "All

I can say is that I felt stronger than I've ever felt before. A lot stronger."

LOCATION: CLASSIFIED (TOP-SECRET MEDICAL LABORATORY)

Pavel and Petro were back in the laboratory, running more tests on Tovarich. Tovarich lifted some weights, just like when he was tested before receiving the formula. This time, Tovarich found them even easier to lift. It was like someone replaced the weights with balloons. As he stood there effortlessly repeating his weight lifts, Pavel took notes nearby. "You've gotten even stronger," Pavel noted. "It seems you can lift even more weights than last time." Next, they had Tovarich run on the treadmill. Like before, they started with him walking at a brisk pace. Petro operated the controls, gradually increasing the speed. Soon Tovarich was running. Petro kept increasing the speed of the treadmill. Pavel walked over and looked at the readouts on the display panel. Tovarich was running at the speed of a car. Pavel was amazed by what he saw. "This is incredible," he noted. "If I were to challenge you to a race—you on foot, me in a car—I honestly couldn't say who would win." Following this, they checked his pulse and blood pressure—both were normal. Petro then tried to take a blood sample, but the needle simply broke when he pressed it into Tovarich's skin.

"Incredible," Petro remarked. Both Pavel and Tovarich looked at the broken needle in Petro's hand, too stunned for words. "I wonder," Petro said out loud.

"You wonder what?" Pavel asked.

Petro walked over to a nearby drawer in a corner desk. Reaching inside, he pulled out a small revolver. "I have a theory," he replied as he turned to Tovarich, aimed the gun directly at him, and pulled the trigger. Pavel backed off, frightened, while Tovarich quickly rose to his feet. The bullet flew out of the barrel and struck Tovarich directly in the chest. Under ordinary circumstances, Tovarich would have been killed right then and there. Instead, the bullet simply bounced off his chest. Tovarich felt the bullet's impact on his body, but it was only a minor sensation, as if someone grabbed a tiny pebble and tossed it at him. Reacting on instinct, Tovarich raced over to Petro so fast it almost looked as if he instantly teleported. With lightning-fast reflexes, Tovarich yanked the gun out of Petro's hand. Petro staggered back nervously. "Forgive me! I wasn't trying to kill you, honest! I was certain that the bullet wouldn't harm you! I SWEAR!"

Tovarich glared at Petro while Pavel motioned toward the gun now in Tovarich's hand. Tovarich's anger quickly turned to surprise when he looked at the gun clenched firmly in his hand. In his anger, Tovarich squeezed his hand tightly, accidentally crushing the gun in the process. Tovarich loosened his grip and stared at the mangled gun in his hand. It was as if the gun had been placed in a trash compactor. He had crushed and deformed it so much that it could no longer fire a shot. Tovarich looked up at Pavel.

An astounded Pavel could only shake his head and say, "I can only assume the formula you were given may still be increasing your natural abilities."

"What's in that formula?" Tovarich asked.

"I honestly don't know," Pavel confessed. "General Duboshnev had it prepared for me. He wouldn't tell me what was in it."

LOCATION: CENTRAL MEETING ROOM, THE CITADEL

General Duboshnev sat with the Premiere and other high-ranking members of the government and top military brass. They were discussing the incident that happened during the parade.

"Someone tried to use our military to kill us," the Premier angrily shouted. He banged his fist on the large oak table, "I want to know who and why!"

The head of the ministry of intelligence placed a folder labelled "top secret" on the table. "According to our investigation, it seemed someone hacked into the tanks' computer controls and remotely controlled them."

"Obviously," the Premier scowled at him. "Does your report happen to mention who's responsible for this?"

The minister hesitated for a minute before muttering, "No."

General Duboshnev spoke up, "It had to be an inside job. Who else could hack our military's computer systems? Someone who knows those systems inside and out."

The minister of intelligence spoke up, "Doctor Pavel Alexandrovich Ulyanov and Doctor Petro Volkov managed to stop the tanks from destroying the Citadel," he opened the folder and showed them the documents inside. "It seems someone downloaded a malware program that allowed the tanks to be remotely controlled. It was a security feature we've been developing in the event that any of our troops decided to mutiny and use our weapons against us; we could use such a program to remotely take control of tanks, aircraft, and so on to prevent our weapons from falling into enemy hands."

"Which, ironically, is exactly what just happened," Duboshnev pointed out.

"Are you saying our military is plotting against us?" the Premier bellowed.

"Could they be plotting some sort of coup?" another minister asked.

The minister of intelligence shrugged sheepishly, "If they are, they've covered their tracks well. We're still investigating this."

"Could the Nihilists be behind this?" Duboshnev asked.

"Possibly," the minister admitted. "We've got hundreds of spies, agents, and informants all over the country, monitoring everyone for possible subversive behaviour. We know for certain that whoever did this was smart enough to bypass the various security programs and software in our systems. They're either a tech genius or quite familiar with our systems." With that, the meeting quickly fell into an ominous silence. The Premier and various aides looked around suspiciously, unsure who they could trust. If there were spies and saboteurs in the government, there was no telling who could be trusted. After several minutes of silence, General Duboshnev finally spoke.

"For now, I think it best that we keep this information on a need-to-know basis," he said. "If anyone finds out, it will cause panic and make the rest of the government, not to mention the public, less likely to trust us, and whoever these criminals are will only go deeper into hiding in an attempt to cover their tracks. Besides," he added, "the last thing we need right now is to let suspicion turn to paranoia, with various government officials hurling baseless accusations at one another." The others looked around and murmured in reluctant agreement.

3

Location: Lenin International Airport

The Liberator didn't like it. After the attack during the military parade, he felt it was unwise for the Premier to be out in the open, exposed, vulnerable. The Premier of Ruthenia and a handful of aides were flying to the Republic of Helvetica in central Europe to attend a summit of world leaders. Most of the world's nations held Ruthenia and its Premier in contempt. Ever since he was a small child, Tovarich had been taught about the enemies of the people and how they didn't deserve mercy. Now the leaders of those so-called "free nations" dared to accuse Ruthenia of human rights violations. The Liberator felt nothing but contempt for them. They had the gall to accuse his nation of oppressing people while capitalist nations allowed large corporations to exploit their workers—nations where less than ten percent of the population had more wealth than the rest of the world combined. The Liberator noted the hypocrisy. It always amazed him. *You're all too eager to call out other countries for their appalling behaviour, yet whenever someone else points out your hypocrisy, you suddenly have dozens of excuses as to why it's okay when you're doing it!* he thought. The irony is that he, like many officials of the country, was also guilty of the very thing he was accusing the western nations of doing.

After the incident at the parade, the Liberator insisted on personally going with the Premier to the summit. However, all the parties quickly shot this down, insisting that his presence there would only make the other nations uneasy. Thus, the Liberator, flanked by a small group of half a dozen armed soldiers, simply escorted the Premier and his aides to the airport to ensure he safely boarded the plane for Helvetica. While Tovarich didn't like it, he did see the logic in their reasoning. He knew that once word of his genetic enhancements got out, the other nations of the world would be plunged into panic. If he were to attend a summit of world leaders, the other nations would undoubtedly see it as Ruthenia trying to intimidate them into submission. Thus, they would more likely escalate hostilities. There were times when it was better to let diplomacy handle situations than brute force. Tovarich had no wish to start another world war. He doubted even he could single-handily fight off entire armies. However, he couldn't help but wonder how many other nations had similar people who were "enhanced" like him. He recalled a rumour about a woman from Oyashima with strange abilities. A woman with pink eyes and two pupils per eye who called herself a...Taman Knight, if he recalled correctly. Some claimed she was an alien from another world, while others assumed she was part of a similar experiment in eugenics as he was.

The sound of the aircraft's turbines starting up snapped him back to his immediate surroundings. The Premier and his aides approached the Liberator, shook his hand and thanked him for safely escorting him to the runway.

"You're certain you don't want me to come along, sir?" the Liberator asked.

The Premier put a reassuring hand on his shoulder, "I appreciate the offer, son, but you know as well as I do that tensions between us and the other nations are already high enough. It's best not to pour more fuel onto the fire."

The Liberator nodded. He knew he wouldn't change the Premier's mind, but a small part of him was still hopeful. "Have a safe trip, sir," he added.

The Premier and his aides nodded and marched up the stairs boarding the plane. With the door closed, the plane began to taxi toward the runway, preparing to take off. As the Liberator turned to leave, he noticed the soldiers going off in a different direction. Tovarich found this odd as they all rode to the airport in the same car. He hadn't been informed that they'd be taking a different vehicle back. He turned and headed toward them to question where they were going. He could see them talking to each other. They were far enough away that the noise from the jet engines should have drowned out whatever they were saying; however, thanks to Tovarich's genetically enhanced hearing, he could still hear their conversation.

"Is our pilot on board?" one of them asked.

"He's on board," another one confirmed.

"What about when they notice the plane going off course?" a third one asked.

"Our fighter jets are being sent to escort it. Just in case the Premier or his aides manage to regain control," the fourth one reassured his nervous comrade. "We'll just say they've been sent to investigate. To retrieve the plane."

"Relax," the second soldier intervened, "No one's gonna find out. Even if..."

The fourth soldier quickly shushed him, motioning toward the Liberator, who was approaching. It was obvious that they, like most people, didn't know the full extent of his enhanced abilities. Thus, they were gambling that he hadn't been able to hear their conversation. They gambled wrong.

"What's this about the plane going off course?" he demanded. The soldiers simply stared nervously at each other. Just as Tovarich suspected, they didn't know that his hearing had been improved. Reaching out, he grabbed the nearest soldier by the collar and yanked him close so that their faces were only inches apart. "I asked a question," he demanded.

Acting on instinct, the soldiers drew their guns and aimed them directly at him. The Liberator, reacting with enhanced speed, strength, and reflexes, used the soldier he was still holding onto as a melee weapon, swinging him at the others to swat them away like flies. The soldier he was holding onto desperately tried to break free of the Liberator's iron grip, but it was no good. The Liberator noticed the plane taxiing down the runway, preparing to take off. Tossing the soldier aside, he turned toward the plane. The other soldiers tackled him, trying to hold him back, but he easily tossed them aside. He began running toward the plane. The odds of him making it before it gained speed and took off would have been impossible for an ordinary person, but an ordinary person didn't have their DNA souped-up as he did.

As the plane began to pick up speed, so did the Liberator. Like when he ran on the treadmill during his medical exams, he ran faster and faster. Tovarich couldn't help but wonder if he really could beat a car in a race. The answer came soon enough. The plane moved faster too. Gaining enough speed for it to take off, faster than even a car could travel. Yet, the Liberator was not only able to keep up; he was actually gaining on it. The plane suddenly began to lift off the ground, just as the Liberator reached under the landing gear. Reacting on instinct, he leapt up into the air, jumping higher than ever before and managed to grab hold of the landing gear. He managed to climb on board just as the landing gear began closing. Tovarich had heard stories of people trying to sneak on board planes by climbing through the landing gear, only to get crushed to death. But then again, most people wouldn't have survived being run over by a tank either.

Inside the plane, the Premier and his aides were sitting down and going over their itinerary for their visit. Two armed guards stood at the front of the plane. As far as anyone knew, they were simply there for security. The truth, however, was that these two and the pilot were actually members of the Nihilist movement. Their goal was to kidnap the Premier, take him to a remote location, and hold him hostage until the government of Ruthenia agreed to their demands. One of the aides noticed both guards were carrying AK-15 assault rifles.

"Is that really necessary?" she asked. "It seems a little like overkill."

"After what happened at the parade, one can never be too careful, ma'am," the guard replied nonchalantly.

As if to prove their point, they were distracted by the sound of banging coming from directly beneath the floor. The guards turned and looked at each other. Neither of them knew what exactly it was, but they had a feeling someone had discovered their plan. Reacting on instinct, they decided to spring into action.

"A stowaway!" one shouted.

"Probably another terrorist," the other one lied. Both guards figured it was a government agent who learned of their plan and snuck on board, trying to stop them. The guards looked at each other and nodded. They decided their best course of action was simply shoot to kill. "Stay here!" the guard told the Premier and his aides. Before they could check it out, the door to the back of the plane opened and out stepped the Liberator.

The Premier and his aides stood up in shock. "How did you get on board?" the Premier asked.

"I climbed in through the landing gear, into the wheel well," he replied. "I then forced my way up, through the floor and into that room back there."

"Why would you do that?" the Premier demanded.

"Because I have reason to believe this plane isn't going to Helvetica," he answered. "I overheard some guards talking on the ground, mentioning that the plane would go off course." He then turned his attention to the two guards. He noticed how nervous they both looked. He could almost hear their hearts racing in their chest. "The guards on the tarmac mentioned that 'their pilot was onboard.' You two wouldn't happen to know anything about that, would you?"

The Premier and his aides turned toward the two guards. Despite the relatively comfortable temperature inside the cabin, everyone noticed how the two guards were both sweating profusely.

"Sir," one of the guards spoke directly to the Premier, "I regret to inform you of this, but we have reason to believe that the Liberator is secretly working with enemy foreign agents. As a result, we've been forced to take a different route to deliver you to a more secure location." This was, of course, a lie. No one had anticipated the Liberator would have caught up to the plane as it was taking off, and they certainly hadn't figured on him making it into the plane. While there had been many reported incidents of people stowing away on planes by hiding in the wheel well, the lack of oxygen, coupled with low air pressure and temperature, meant most people who attempted such a feat didn't survive, even assuming they weren't simply crushed to death when the landing gear retracted.

"And why wasn't I notified of this?" the Premier asked doubtfully.

"It was for your own safety, sir," the other guard lied. "We couldn't risk him finding out," he nervously gestured toward the Liberator.

"Then why did the soldiers on the ground say they were sending fighter jets to escort it? Just in case the Premier or his aides managed to regain control?" he demanded.

The guards looked at each other nervously. One of them turned to the Premier. "He's lying, sir," the guard stammered.

"You're the ones who are lying!" the Liberator shouted as he slowly moved toward them. "Who are you? Who sent you? Are you part of the group that hacked control of the tanks and made them attack the Citadel?"

With their cover blown, the guards aimed their guns at the Liberator and opened fire. Like when Petro tested Tovarich by shooting him with the handgun back in the lab, the bullets struck the Liberator straight in the chest, torso, and head, only to bounce right off him. They stopped firing and stared at him with pure dread. Even Tovarich was slightly surprised by this. Unlike Petro's "test," these were full automatic AK-15 assault rifles, much more powerful than a simple revolver.

I guess I shouldn't be surprised, Tovarich thought. *After all, I was crushed by a tank only a few days ago, yet I'm still alive. Compared to that, being shot by AK-15s is nothing.* He moved toward the Nihilists. Not knowing what to do, they simply aimed their guns at him and opened fire again. It was a futile attempt, but then again, they probably weren't expecting this, so they didn't exactly have many options. However, the Liberator wasn't concerned about himself; he was worried about the Premier. If they continued firing, there was a possibility some of the bullets might ricochet off him and strike the Premiere or puncture holes in the cabin. Fortunately, the Premier and his aides took cover behind some chairs. Thus, the Nihilists continued firing until they exhausted all their ammo. Panicking and acting out of desperation, one of the Nihilists swung his rifle at the Liberator like a bat, hoping that he could bludgeon him to death. This time, Liberator willingly did nothing. He was now confident that he was in no danger. Thus, the rifle struck him in the side of his head, only to break upon impact. The Nihilist just stood there paralyzed with fear. The Liberator stood there, giving him a cold, hard stare, allowing his opponent a moment to realize that it was truly futile. The other Nihilist, either bravely or foolishly, pulled out a survival egress knife, the kind used by military personnel if they needed to escape a downed aircraft and survive in the wilderness. He charged the Liberator, trying in vain to slash and stab him with it. Like before, Liberator did nothing. He wanted to show his opponent that it was futile. Thus, he slashed at the Liberator's throat, but the blade did nothing, not even scratch his skin. Next, he tried to stab him in the chest. However, the blade simply broke upon impact. Raising his right arm, the Liberator delivered a backhand slap to the man's face. The man flew backwards, slamming into the far wall of the cabin, before collapsing dead on the floor. However, the Liberator wasn't sure if the impact of his hand or his head hitting the cabin wall delivered the killing blow. Not that it mattered to the Liberator, this man was an enemy of the people, so he got what he deserved as far as Tovarich was concerned.

The Liberator turned his attention to the other Nihilist who had tried to bludgeon him with the assault rifle. Realizing how truly screwed he was, he fell to his knees, "Please, don't kill me!" he begged. "Have mercy!"

"Enemies of the people don't deserve mercy," the Liberator coldly reminded him, quoting a phrase that had been drilled into the heads of Ruthenians all their lives. With his genetically enhanced reflexes, he grabbed the man by his neck and snapped it like a twig with little effort.

Turning his attention back to the Premier, who peeked out from behind his chair, the Liberator asked, "Are you all right, sir?"

The Premier nodded uneasily.

"Stay here," the Liberator instructed before heading to the cockpit. The Liberator entered the cockpit. Grabbing the pilot by his right arm, the Liberator yanked him out of his chair. "Turn this plane around and land right now!" he barked.

The pilot just grinned smugly, "Or what? You'll kill me? If I land the plane, I'll be arrested, and then they'll sentence me to death anyway. Besides, even if you do kill me, there would be no one left to fly the plane, so your threat is meaningless!"

The Liberator glared at him. The man was right. If he did comply and land the plane, he'd be arrested and given a show trial where a guilty verdict would already be rendered before the trial even began. "So what you're saying is I should just kill you right here and now?" he threatened.

"Look out the window," the pilot motioned. The Liberator turned his head to see two fighter jets, one on either side, flanking the plane.

"You've hijacked this plane; you obviously want the Premier alive," the Liberator deduced. "Tell those pilots to stand down. If they open fire, you'll kill your hostage."

"What makes you think that wasn't part of our plan?" the pilot bluffed.

"Why go to all this trouble just to kill him?" the Liberator figured. "There are many easier ways you could have finished off the Premier. Why go to all this trouble if you just wanted him dead?"

"You're right," the pilot admitted, "we hoped to take him alive and force him to submit to our demands. But since that's obviously no longer an option, we might as well just shoot the plane down."

"If they shoot down the plane, you die too," the Liberator argued. He had hoped that might compel the pilot to cooperate.

The pilot just shrugged, "I'm dead either way. And soon, you'll be too!"

"Will I? A tank at the parade ran me over, and I survived without even a scratch," the Liberator replied. After having survived that, he was certain that he'd survive being shot down by another plane.

"Can the Premier also make that claim?" the pilot asked.

The Liberator silently cursed as he released his grip on the pilot. He had hoped that fear would cause the pilot to forget about the Premier. The more the Liberator thought it over, there was only one way to end this.

Meanwhile, the pilot turned and grabbed the cockpit radio. He contacted the fighter jets following him, "The Liberator IS HERE! OPEN FIRE!"

The Liberator grabbed the pilot and, with his genetically enhanced might, flung him across the cockpit. The pilot smashed into the far wall with such an impact that he was killed instantly. The Liberator wasn't concerned about that. As far as he was concerned, that man was an enemy of the people. He could still recall the lesson the state had repeatedly drilled into his head since he first became a secret police officer: *Enemies of the people don't deserve compassion or mercy.* Thus, he felt no remorse over killing a suspected terrorist. Besides, he had more important things to worry about right now. He grabbed the radio, "This is the Liberator, do not open fire! Repeat, DO NOT OPEN FIRE!" Unfortunately, his words fell on deaf ears.

The fighter jets aimed at the plane and opened fire. Thanks to his genetically enhanced hearing, the Liberator could hear the bullets as they perforated the plane's jet engines. He heard the engines shutting down. He looked at the control. He debated taking control of the plane himself but quickly dismissed that. Although he had briefly served in the army before joining the secret police, he had no experience or knowledge of how to fly a plane. He gazed at the various dials and controls in front of him. While his intelligence had been enhanced along with his physical prowess, even he couldn't figure out how to fly a plane without engines in a matter of seconds, especially while being shot at by other planes. Besides, there was also the fact that the fighter jets had missiles on them. If one of them shot at the plane, it was all over. While the Liberator figured he could survive, the others wouldn't. Besides, where could they go? If they jumped out of the plane, they would fall to their deaths. Even the Liberator wasn't certain he could survive a fall from these heights. While he could use the emergency parachutes the plane had been equipped with, there was the risk that the fighter jets would simply aim at the parachutes and pick them off easily. The sound of an explosion rocking the plane caused him to lose balance temporarily. The Liberator slammed into the right side of the plane. He could smell smoke. It was just as he feared; they were firing missiles at the plane.

The Liberator raced up to the co-pilot's seat and grabbed the radio, "This is the Liberator," he shouted, "STOP FIRING! REPEAT, STOP FIRING! YOUR ALLIES HAVE ALL BEEN KILLED! STAND DOWN! YOU'LL KILL THE PREMIER!" He tried again to convince them that their plans would be for naught if they killed their intended hostage.

He heard a voice on the other end of the radio, "So be it," it responded.

A feeling of dread suddenly came over the Liberator, "Who is this?" he demanded.

"Just another 'enemy of the people,'" the voice replied sarcastically. It was just as Tovarich feared; the fighter jets were more Nihilists. Their plan was obviously to kidnap the Premier and hold him hostage until their demands were met. He figured the soldiers on the ground were in on it too and had told their fellow traitors that the Liberator boarded the plane. His unexpected arrival threw their plans into disarray. Thus, instead of taking anyone hostage, they were now simply going to kill them all.

The Liberator rushed to the back of the plane, where the Premier and his aides were sitting, wondering what was happening.

"What's going on?" the Premier demanded.

"We need to get off this plane," the Liberator replied, opening the overhead emergency storage compartments. He pulled out some parachutes and tossed them at the Premier and his aides. "Hurry, put these on. We're going to have to jump."

"Are you crazy?" one of the aides asked. "They've got missiles; they'll pick us off easily!"

"If we stay here, they'll just shoot the plane down anyway," he replied.

The aides stopped to consider his words. After all, he had a point: either stay in the plane and get shot down or jump for safety and take the risk. Perhaps there was hope that while they were free-falling, it would make it harder for the fighter jets to lock weapons on such small, moving targets before they pulled the parachutes. The sound of another explosion, one that shook the whole cabin, made the decision for them. They were all thrown to the ground while the plane dipped its nose, diving down toward the earth. The aide looked out the window only to see a flaming piece of the broken wing spiralling off in the distance. They quickly put on the parachutes.

"Stand back," the Liberator told them. He threw himself at the sidewall with all his might, slamming into it with his superhuman strength. It made a huge dent in the sidewall. Half expecting it to simply break off, the Liberator balled his hands into fists and began pounding the wall in frustration, desperately hoping he could smash a hole through it. He stared at the wall intently with rage, as if hoping the fury in his eyes would burn a hole right through it. Suddenly, as if something deep inside him answered, he felt a strange feeling swell up in his eyes. He watched in shock as bright beams of crimson red energy fired from his eyes, striking the wall with the force of a grenade. The wall blasted apart, forming a large hole for them to jump out. He stared at the hole with amazement.

The Premier and the rest of his aides stood behind him in complete shock. While the Premier knew about the Liberator's genetic enhancements, he wasn't aware of the full extent of his powers. "How...how did you do that?" he asked.

"I'm...not sure..." the Liberator wondered. Unfortunately, he didn't have time to figure it out. He turned to face the Premier, "Now's not the time. We've got to go! You first, sir!" Taking charge of the situation, he grabbed the Premier and carefully pulled him toward the opening. After briefly showing him how to pull the parachute, he pushed the Premier out of the hole in the plane. He then did the same for his two aides. Finally, with all the passengers off, the Liberator jumped out himself.

A strange sensation came over the Liberator as he was free-falling. He couldn't quite explain or even understand it, but it felt like his body was trying to fight the pull of gravity. Instinctively, he seemed to be slowing his descent somehow, despite not having pulled his parachute yet. Looking down, he saw the Premier and his aides had already pulled their chutes and were safely floating toward the ground. That's when a terrifying sight hit his eyes. The fighter planes turned and aimed their guns at the parachutes. The Liberator was afraid of this. In the back of his mind, he realized that with them parachuting down, they offered an easy target for the Nihilists. But what other option did he have? If they had stayed inside the plane, the fighters would have just continued shooting the plane until it went down. Even if the Liberator managed to take control of it, how could he possibly land it safely with two hostile planes continuing to fire upon it? Unfortunately for him, he didn't have the luxury of worrying about what he should have done. All he could do was watch helplessly as one of the parachutes became ripped with bullet holes.

NO! he screamed in his mind, *NO! DAMMIT TO HELL!* He turned to look up at the plane firing upon it. Immense fury built up behind his eyes, just like when he blasted a hole in the wall. Like before, he watched as the plane was struck by another large beam of crimson red energy, causing it to explode before his eyes. *Another side effect of the genetic enhancements,* he figured. However, he didn't have time to ponder it. Turning to the other plane, he saw it turning to face him. It opened fire. He felt the bullets strike him directly in the chest, but like before, they just bounced off him. That's when he noticed something even more strange. He was hovering in the air. He hadn't deployed his parachute, yet he wasn't falling. He just seemed to be hovering in place, defying gravity. *This just keeps getting weirder and weirder,* he thought. Distracted by this, he failed to notice the fighter jet fire a missile directly at him. The explosive force of the missile managed to knock him away. He felt himself spinning from the impact and the explosion, but he still wasn't falling. He imagined this was what it must have felt like to be a cosmonaut in space. He managed to regain control of his body and righted himself. Like before, he stared directly at the plane, focusing his fury on it, trying to fire his optic beams at the plane. Once again, thick, wavy crimson red beams of energy shot from his eye sockets, striking the enemy plane with the speed of a laser and the concussive force of a missile. The Liberator watched as the second plane exploded before his eyes.

The terrorists and their hijacked fighter planes had been eliminated, but he didn't have time to celebrate. Turning his attention back to the Premier and his aides, he noticed they were still plummeting toward the ground. Cursing himself for getting distracted, he turned himself upside down and began rocketing toward the ground with the speed of the missile that shot him earlier. He noticed that two of the parachutes had been shredded by the bullets, but the third seemed unscathed. Obviously, the Nihilists didn't expect the Liberator to counterattack as he did; thus, they didn't have time to target the third parachute. The only question remaining was whether he could rescue the falling people before they splattered on the ground. He wasn't sure which two were falling; he only hoped he could get to them in time. Diving straight down, he caught the first—one of the Premier's aides. Unfortunately, he was already too late. It seemed a few of the bullets punctured his skull, killing him instantly. Turning his attention to the other falling parachute, he could see her waving her arms and legs frantically; at least, he hoped it was her and not the wind causing her lifeless limbs to flail about. As he raced toward her, he moved the dead body to his right arm. He debated tossing it aside but quickly discarded that idea. He didn't want to risk having it fall on something or someone. There was no point in causing any more damage or death than necessary. Swooping down, he wrapped his left arm around her waist and held her close. Turning himself right side up, he began to slow his descent. Soon it was as though the parachute on his back had been deployed, even though it hadn't. Slowing his descent even further, the Liberator and his two passengers gently touched down in a grassy field not too far from a small rural village.

"Are you all right, ma'am?" he asked as he gently released the female aide.

She nodded as the Liberator turned and carefully lowered the body of the other aide onto the ground.

"Wait here," he told her as he turned and looked up to the third parachute, the Premier, still floating toward the ground. Moving as if he were preparing to jump, he rocketed up toward the Premier. The aide could only watch in awe. She recalled how she had pulled her chute and began to slowly descend when she suddenly felt her descent quicken. She had looked up to see her parachute had been ripped open with bullet holes. The next thing she knew, she was free-falling once again. She figured she was going to die, if not from the bullets, then when she hit the ground. She never anticipated that the Liberator would swoop down to save her, flying around like someone out of a comic book. Yet that was exactly what happened. She looked up. She could barely make out the Liberator grabbing the Premier and flying him down to the ground, removing the parachute and tossing it aside. Soon the Premier was safely on the ground with the Liberator and his surviving aide. "Are you all right, sir?" the Liberator asked.

The Premier nodded, "Thanks to you, son! But how exactly did you do all those things? You appeared to fire some sort of energy beams from your eyes, making those planes explode on impact. How did you do that?"

The Liberator shrugged with confusion, "Honestly, I don't know. What was in that formula that genetically enhanced me?"

4

News of the Liberator's success rescuing the Premier and foiling the Nihilist kidnapping plot soon spread across the country. By government decree, the media had ramped up propaganda, not to mention Liberator merchandise, to an excited public. As news of his newfound powers soon spread, the public reaction was both swift and divided. While officially, the public was supposed to show support for their new "invincible" hero, only some felt such feelings. For many others, they only acted that way when directly asked what their opinion on the Liberator was. In truth, some felt an overwhelming sense of dread. Though most would never admit it, many secretly resented their new state-sponsored superhero. To them, he was less a symbol of the might and righteousness of their socialist state and more a symbol of totalitarian oppression, the indestructible hero who would crush all dissidents under his heel. And it wasn't just in Ruthenia that people had these fears. When word soon spread outside of the country, the reaction was swift. Many nations officially condemned Ruthenia for creating genetically-enhanced humans. Since there was no official record of any nation practising genetic engineering before, there were no laws on it. Thus, many nations scrambled to look into this to determine how to handle a new and "improved" breed of human. One such country that showed interest was the nation of Usonia.

If Ruthenia was a symbol of totalitarian oppression, then the Republic of Usonia was its counterpart, a symbol of the land of the free. At least, that was their official claim. Despite their boasting of being the land of the free, where all men are created equal, the truth, like in many other nations, was that Usonia often didn't practise what it preached. Wealth inequality, as well as racial inequality, not to mention discrimination based on gender and sexual orientation, were problems that still plagued the nation. It was a divided nation where people of various races, classes, religions, gender, and sexual orientation were supposed to live together as "one nation under God." However, there were often petty arguments over politics, religious beliefs, race, and so on. Nowhere was this divide more reflected than in the nation's capital. Like many democratic countries, multiple political parties would often hold power only to lose it in the next election. Some liberals wanted to pass legislation that would help the working class, and there were conservatives who favoured tax cuts for the wealthy and saw the average Usonian as pawns to be exploited for their own wealth. There were moderates on both sides willing to help the average Usonian unless, of course, corporate lobbyists offered them a large campaign contribution to kill such bills in the senate, and there were those farther to both the left and the right. Some on the left felt the government didn't go far enough and wanted a more fair and equal society akin to democratic socialism, if not outright communism. Conversely, those on the right tended to lean more toward fascism.

In the Capitol Building, where the various members of Congress and senators met to discuss policy, pass bills into law, or more often, obstruct the other party from passing bills into law, one senator was secretly meeting with a member of the country's military to discuss the matter of the Liberator. His name was Ronald Alan Whitman. He was a staunchly conservative senator, elected by playing on the voters' fears of "woke" liberals plotting to take over the country with secret help from Ruthenia. He was elected and supported by large corporations with the promise of tax cuts for the wealthy and looser government regulations regarding health and safety, plus the environment. He was elected and also supported by the ignorant voters on the right who bought into his talking points. It was senator Whitman who helped slash funding to education because it would turn Usonia's children into "woke liberal commies" that would one day take over the country and destroy "wholesome family values and traditions." While a part of him truly believed this, another part of him was more realistic. He knew it was necessary to keep the people ignorant. After all, studies had shown that well-educated citizens tended to overwhelmingly vote liberal in elections. The smarter the people got, the less likely they were to buy into his political talking points, meaning he could kiss his chances of winning re-election goodbye. And if that happened, he wouldn't be able to pass laws that granted large corporations, like the various ones he owned stock in, tax breaks, and other benefits. The last thing he wanted was for Usonia to end up a communist country like Ruthenia, which is what he feared if too many progressives on the left kept getting elected. It was because of Ruthenia, and more importantly, their new state-sponsored hero, the Liberator, that he was meeting today with one of the country's highest-ranking generals.

General Thomas Flagg was the Usonian counterpart to Ruthenia's General Duboshnev. Like Duboshnev, he was a high-ranking general in the military. Also, like Duboshnev, he was in his late fifties yet still cut an imposing figure. Even under his military uniform, adorned with various medals, he was still a well-muscled figure who arguably could take on and defeat a man half his age in a fight. He had short brownish-grey hair cut in a short military style and cold steel-like blue eyes. This was his most prominent feature. His eyes seemed to have an almost hypnotic-like quality. They gave him a piercing gaze that could excite his followers while terrorizing his opponents. The difference between the two was that Duboshnev was a member of his country's communist party, whereas Flagg was a hard-line conservative and die-hard anti-communist with, as some would say, an obsessive zeal to destroy any potential threats to his country—an obsessive zeal that could more accurately be called irrational paranoia. Like many Usonians on the right, Flagg tended to reject science and fact in favour of radical conspiracy theories which had little to no basis in reality. In a more progressive society, he probably would have been living on government welfare while receiving treatment for his delusions. However, in Usonia, such government programs didn't exist. Many on the right, including Flagg himself, would decry such acts as "communism" and "government overreach." Ironically, people like General Flagg had no objections to using "government overreach" to enforce their right-wing propaganda on their own populace and using their own constitution's "freedom of speech" to justify all their hate speech and baseless attacks on the left while using whatever loophole they could in the constitution to silence those on the left, whom they frequently attacked for "unpatriotic behaviour." That very same constitution, plus push back from more liberal elements of society and government, were the only things that prevented people like Flagg and many right-wing politicians from turning Usonia from "the land of the free' into a fascist dictatorship. Unfortunately, it only poured more fuel on the fire and was often used by the right as "proof" that the "liberals" and "progressives" were trying to turn the country into a communist dictatorship like Ruthenia. This was why the General was meeting with Senator Whitman to discuss this threat. A threat that thanks to the Liberator, they were now convinced was even greater.

"According to our reports, he even survived being run over by a tank," General Flagg told the Senator, reading a report of the incident during the Liberation Day parade. Thanks to various spies and informants Usonia had operating in Ruthenia, information that the Ruthenian government worked hard to keep the public ignorant of still managed to make its way out of the country and into the hands of people like Flagg.

Senator Whitman looked over another report from some agents in Ruthenia, "According to this one, this Liberator now can fly and shoot 'energy beams' from his eyes."

"While none of our spies have seen these things first hand, they've read the official, classified documents that verify this," Flagg reported.

"Aww hell..." Senator Whitman rubbed his forehead. "Just what we need, some super-powered commie flying around that we can't destroy. What's to stop them from just sending him over here and taking over the whole country?"

"We still have our nukes," Flagg replied. "I doubt even he could survive a direct nuclear assault."

"Unfortunately, neither would we, General," Whitman reminded him. This was one of the differences between the Senator and the General. Senator Whitman had no objections to Usonia going to war; after all, he held stock in numerous weapons manufacturing corporations. Whenever Usonia had gone to war in the past, he made a fortune in defence contracts. However, he had no wish to start a nuclear war, especially when the target was hovering directly over his home. He may have been a greedy war profiteer, but he still knew there was no profit to be made in blowing up your own house. On the other hand, General Flagg was a soldier through and through. To him, the need to fight and, if necessary, die for one's country was sacrosanct. In his view, everyone would and should be willing to sacrifice themselves for the good of Usonia, even if it meant throwing their lives away for no practical reason. In his mind, it was better to die in a scorched earth, murder/suicide battle than surrender or even use peace and diplomacy to solve their problems. "However, there is another option," the senator added. "If we could figure out how they created the Liberator, how they managed to genetically enhance him..."

"...we could create our own version," the General deduced, finishing Senator Whitman's sentence. "Our own counterpart to the Liberator. One loyal to us. One who could defeat him in battle."

Senator Whitman nodded, "Unfortunately, I doubt the government would go along with it. Tampering with people's genes. I admit I'm not particularly fond of the idea myself. It seems to go against the laws of God."

"Those godless commies don't care about such things!" Flagg angrily slammed his fist down on the table, leaving a slight dent in the wood. "Why, they don't even believe in God! They've turned their backs on God, so God has turned his back on them! So, it's our sacred duty from God to do the same thing. It's what Jesus would do!" Unfortunately, the irony, or perhaps hypocrisy of what he was saying, had been completely lost on both of them. Like many of the religious right, they would often invoke God and Jesus in their arguments to justify acting in a way that went against everything both stood for.

"You'll get no argument from me there, General," Whitman reassured him. "However, I'm not so sure I can convince my fellow senators or members of Congress to go along with it. And even if I could, I doubt the President would go along with it. Even if we could pass a bill legalizing genetic engineering, the President would most likely use his executive veto to shoot it down."

"That's what we get for electing a liberal commie for a President," Flagg lamented.

Senator Whitman nodded in agreement. As far as either of them was concerned, anyone who was a member of the Liberal Democratic Party of Usonia was a "commie," even if they were so moderate, you could easily mistake them for a conservative. This was their narrow view of the world: conservatives could do no wrong, while liberals were pure evil. The Senator leaned over his desk so his face was only a few inches away from Flagg's. He whispered, "I'll get some legislation passed that will increase funding to the military for 'research into treating soldiers' injuries.' Use that and begin working on creating our own counterpart to this Liberator."

Flagg nodded in agreement.

"Make sure no one knows what you're doing," Whitman added. "This project is strictly on a need-to-know basis. If anyone asks, it's helping our troops deal with post-traumatic stress, re-growing lost limbs, or something like that. Just make sure no one finds out."

LOCATION: THE INTELLECTUAL'S HEADQUARTERS, CITY OF MOVOGORSKY, RUTHENIA

The Intellectual sat in his office watching the state news broadcast. It told the people how the Nihilists tried to take the Premier and his aides hostage by hijacking their plane when the Liberator showed up to stop them. The broadcast depicted the Liberator in a flattering light while simultaneously portraying the Nihilists as cowards and terrorists. Upon mentioning the Liberator's newfound powers, the news anchor seemed to go out of his way to preach as if such powers were some divine gift to the people of Ruthenia as if there were some communist god who sent the Liberator to Ruthenia like he was some divine saviour. The Intellectual couldn't help but find it ironic that for a country that officially outlawed religion, they would go and treat their new hero, like most of their political figures, as if they were god-like themselves. Of course, the Intellectual saw right through this propaganda. He knew that the Liberator had been genetically modified. Despite his group, the Nihilists, being discovered and arrested, he still had a large network of spies, informants and double agents working within the state. No amount of information, no matter how top secret, was kept from him. That is, except for these new powers the Liberator had developed. While he knew about the formula given to the Liberator, he had still been unable to learn all about it—how exactly it gave him these powers and, more importantly, why. The Intellectual didn't like this. He prided himself on his intelligence, knowledge, and keen analytical mind. He always boasted about how he could accurately predict any event's possible outcomes, no matter how many variables. However, these variables were ones he failed to account for. That gnawed at him. Ever since the kidnapping had failed, he had been going over the incident in his mind, replaying it again and again, trying to figure out what he missed. He was so preoccupied with it that he didn't even notice one of his minions entering the room.

"Excuse me, sir," he spoke nervously, afraid of incurring the Intellectual's wrath. If there was one thing the Intellectual didn't like, it was when people interrupted his train of thought. But this time, he was too obsessed with the mission's failure to notice.

"How could I have not seen it?" he asked no one. He was simply thinking out loud. "I calculated every variable, every outcome! I should have seen it!"

"Uh...forgive my interruption, sir," his minion said timidly, "but they've discovered our agents working in the air force."

But again, the Intellectual wasn't listening, "These new variables will throw off my whole calculations! This changes everything!"

"They're being interrogated right now," his minion continued, "if they discover anything..."

"I must know how this happened!" the Intellectual continued his train of thought, not paying attention to his minion's words. "I must know how he got these powers! I must find out what was in that formula!"

Seeing that his boss wasn't paying attention, the minion decided to change the subject, "Why don't we just get our spies in the government to get their hands on that formula that they gave the Liberator?" he offered helpfully.

This managed to get the Intellectual's attention. He turned and gazed intently at his minion, "What did you just say?"

"I'm sorry, boss," his minion stammered, fearing he was in trouble. "I didn't mean to interrupt, honest. I just..."

"Cease your cowardly whining," the Intellectual cut him off. "What was it you said about the formula?"

"I suggested that you get our spies to get their hands on it, then I'm sure with your smarts, you could figure out how the Liberator got those powers of his."

The Intellectual looked at him and smiled, "Of course. I have agents everywhere. Nothing happens in the government without my knowledge."

"Yes, sir!" the minion quickly confirmed. He figured it was best not to point out that the Liberator's new powers happened without his knowledge. "But what about our spies that were captured?"

"Captured?" the Intellectual asked.

"I tried to tell you, sir," he replied. "Our agents at the airport were captured."

The Intellectual gave him a cold, hard gaze, "Make sure they don't say anything. Eliminate them if necessary! And if the state learns anything from them, make sure our other agents gather all the information the state learned and destroys it, so there'll be no record."

LOCATION: TOVARICH'S APARTMENT, CITY OF MOVOGORSKY

Tovarich Revanov was once again sitting in his apartment watching TV while drinking directly from another bottle of vodka. He was watching the same news broadcasts the Intellectual was watching. He couldn't believe what he was hearing, the news anchor praising him as if the

Liberator, the People's Guard was some divine saviour sent by some communist god to deliver the workers and peasants of Ruthenia to salvation. He turned off the TV in disgust. Tovarich had saved the Premiere and his aides; he was a national hero. He should have felt proud, but for some reason, he wasn't. Instead, he couldn't help but feel he wasn't truly a hero. A part of him—a very small part—felt as if his actions only served to justify the brutal totalitarian control the rest of the world accused his government of having over the people of Ruthenia.

Tovarich took another swig from the bottle of vodka, trying in vain to drown these conflicted feelings within himself. Even before becoming the Liberator, the People's Guard, he worked for years as a secret police officer, rooting out enemies of the state, of the people. He had always been taught that such enemies didn't deserve compassion and mercy. As a secret police officer, he had been responsible for the arrests and deaths of many threats to the people. Such things never bothered him before, so why did they bother him now? Could it have been his going undercover as a Nihilist? All that time, all those lies he made about the atrocities of his own government, the passionate arguments he made while posing as a Nihilist; could it be that he was starting to believe his own lies? Or was it something else? Perhaps, deep down inside, a small part of him knew his government was a totalitarian dictatorship that was only concerned about holding on to power at all costs and didn't have the people's best interests at heart. For all those years, he could suppress that nagging doubt in the back of his mind. Perhaps after all those years, he couldn't suppress it anymore. Like an old, worn-down dam halting the flow of water down the river, the pressure had been building up for years. Cracks were starting to form in the dam, causing small leaks of doubt to trickle through. How long before the dam burst and all those repressed feelings, those doubts and insecurities, would come flooding out, with nothing able to stop them? Tovarich downed the last of his vodka and reached for another bottle. Hopefully, he could drown those feelings in a sea of alcohol.

The adventure continues in
Liberator: The People's Guard, Volume 2...

www.ingramcontent.com/pod-product-compliance
Lightning Source LLC
Chambersburg PA
CBHW031357060726
47590CB00007B/2831